MARVEL
AVENGERS
MS. MARVEL'S
FISTS OF
FURY

 Published by Marvel Press, an imprint of Disney Book Group. For information address Marvel Press, 125 West End Avenue, New York, New York 10023.
Printed in the United States of America. First Paperback Edition, October 2017 10 9 8 7 6 5 4 3 2 1 Library of Congress Control Number: 2016932665
FAC-029261-17230 ISBN 978-1-4847-8146-3

Cover illustration by Ron Lim and Caravan Studios
Designed by Kurt Hartman

STARRING MS. MARVEL

BY CALLIOPE GLASS

ILLUSTRATED BY CARAVAN STUDIOS

MARVEL

Los Angeles
New York

FEATURING YOUR FAVORITES
MS. MARVEL
NAKIA
MR. KHAN
THOR
A PET-SHOP OWNER
A WAITRESS
MJOLNIR
A RIDICULOUS
HARD BIOLO
TEST

BRUNO
CHICKEN-BOY
LOCK FOREVER
A SHINY RED BUTTON
THE INVENTOR
HAWKEYE
A CELL PHONE
A BUNCH OF INHUMAN TEENAGERS
AND A LOT OF BIRDS. SO MANY BIRDS.

THE STORY OF MS. MARVEL

Until recently, Jersey City's **Kamala Khan** didn't think she was special. But one night not too long ago, everything changed. Kamala was caught in a mysterious mist, and when she recovered, she realized that her Inhuman powers were suddenly activated. Kamala went from being an ordinary high school student to being **Ms. Marvel**—a Super Hero with the power to stretch, morph, and heal.

Kamala Khan was determined to keep living her life as an ordinary girl—going to school, going to her mosque, and writing Avengers fanfic on the internet. So she hid her Super Hero identity from everyone in her life. But in secret, Kamala began to fight crime as Ms. Marvel. Eventually her friend Bruno found out, and has been in on the secret ever since.

As Ms. Marvel, Kamala was able to fight Super Villains and other supernatural criminals in Jersey City. She used her new powers to become large enough to punch out giant robots, and small enough to climb inside their guts. Basically, she fought a lot of giant robots. But her powers also allowed her to change her shape and to heal faster than ordinary people.

The healing powers came in handy, because

Kamala wasn't the type of hero to stand back and stay safe when things got dangerous. She fought hard, and she got hurt sometimes. But being a hero meant a lot to Kamala—she was determined to help people. So she kept practicing, and kept fighting, and eventually became an unstoppable force for good. Kamala Khan finally became

CHAPTER 1

"Don't be late, don't be late, don't be late," Kamala Khan chanted under her breath.

She walked as fast as she could without actually running. Kamala was on her way to school, and she already had three tardies on her record for the month.

"Stupid criminals, always making me late for school," Kamala muttered. She had her hands full with her schoolwork and her family. Balancing her regular life with her life as the Super Hero

Ms. Marvel was always hard. Sometimes it was more than Kamala could handle. But not today. Today was totally under control.

"So far so good," Kamala said, pausing at a streetlight and checking the time on her phone. "Seven fifty-one. I'm definitely, for sure going to get to school on time. I'm not stopping for anything short of an actual Super Villain."

RRRRRRRIIINNNNNGGG!!!

The quiet morning air was shattered by a loud alarm bell.

"Help!" someone yelled. "My store is being robbed!"

There was a pause, then the person added:

"By a Super Villain!"

With a weary sigh, Kamala ducked into an alley. She hid behind a Dumpster and pulled off her regular clothes, revealing her Ms. Marvel costume.

"Let's do this," Ms. Marvel said. That Super Villain was

going to regret maybe-probably making her late to school.

RRRRRRRRIIIIIINNNNNN—CRUNCH!

Ms. Marvel smashed the alarm bell with her embiggened fist. "I'll replace that," she told the shop owner sheepishly. "It was just making it really hard for me to concentrate."

Then Ms. Marvel stretched one arm

long until she could grab the criminal by the scruff of the neck.

The person she pulled out of the store was wearing a hoodie and a . . . beak?

"Squawk!" she said. **"Squawk, squawk!"**

"I wouldn't exactly call *her* a Super Villain," Ms. Marvel said to the shop owner. "Super Villains don't usually wear Halloween masks."

"Hey!" the bird-girl said, offended. Her eyes lit up and she zapped laser beams at Ms. Marvel, but Ms. Marvel quickly slapped a hand over the girl's eyes.

"Ow!" the girl yelped as she accidentally shot lasers at the insides of her own eyelids.

"Put a tight blindfold on her, and you should be fine," Ms. Marvel told the police, who were arriving on the scene. She handed the bird-girl over to them and hurried back to the alleyway to get her regular clothes back on.

"Don't be late, don't be late, don't be late," Kamala muttered as she jogged toward her school. "Ammi and Abu would be so mad if they knew where I was!"

Kamala hated disappointing her parents. The thought of having to explain another tardy on her report card was enough to make Kamala go from a jog to a sprint.

She ran into the classroom as the bell was ringing and slid into her seat just in time!

Later that day, she saw her friend Bruno at lunch.

YOU LOOK KIND OF FRAZZLED.
EVERYTHING OKAY?

"Yeah, I just had a weird morning," Kamala said. She lowered her voice. Bruno knew about Ms. Marvel, but nobody else at school did. "I foiled a robbery."

"Cool!" Bruno said. "A bank? A hotel? A jewelry store?"

"No," Kamala said. "A pet store. And the girl who was robbing it squawked at me."

"Squawked?" Bruno said.

"And that's not the weirdest part," Kamala said. "She was wearing a bird mask."

"You're right," Bruno said. "That *is* weird. Oh—here comes Nakia!"

Nakia did *not* know about Ms. Marvel, so Kamala and Bruno changed the subject.

"Have you started studying for that big Biology test on Thursday?" Kamala asked Nakia.

"Yeah," Nakia said, "all week. But I need to study more. I can't believe half our grade is based on this one test!"

"I haven't even started studying for it," Kamala admitted. "I'm kind of freaking out."

Nakia stared at her. "You haven't even started?" she said, shocked. "But it's half our grade! What would your parents–?"

"I *know*," Kamala said, glaring at her friend.

Nakia cocked her head. "You've been kind of cranky lately," she said. "Is everything okay?"

Bruno nodded. "I've noticed that, too," he said. "I know you've been really . . . busy." He gave Kamala a knowing look.

"I'm fine," Kamala said. The whole conversation was stressing her out, and she wanted it to be over. So she smiled brightly. "See? Fine. Hey, have you guys been playing *Pork-Bun Go*?"

"Oh my gosh, I finally captured a wild spinach dumpling!" Bruno said, pulling up the game's app on his phone.

Nakia got out her phone. "I don't have any spinach dumplings. But I have eleven shrimp shumais. Want to trade?"

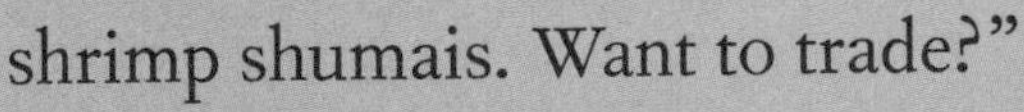

"No way," Bruno said. "But you can have one of my pea shoots."

Kamala watched her friends with a smile firmly fixed on her face. But inside, it was all starting to get to her.

Sometimes Kamala thought she just wasn't cut out for Super Hero-ing.

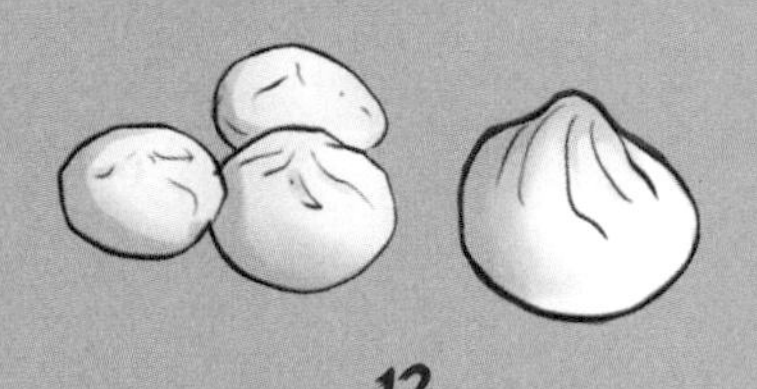

CHAPTER 2

The rest of the day passed by in a blur. Kamala couldn't stop thinking about the big Biology test.

Nakia's been studying for a week already. Kamala absentmindedly passed the basketball to someone on the other team in gym class.

"Hey!" one of Kamala's teammates yelled, but Kamala barely heard him. She was too wrapped up in her worries. *I should have been studying, too. But when? I've been out late fighting crime every night for the last two weeks.*

"You're the worst, Khan," her teammate told Kamala.

Kamala ignored him, but the boy continued, still annoyed. "You're a total—**OOMPH!**"

He was cut off by the basketball bouncing off his head.

Kamala rolled her eyes. *I have to get a grip. There are just too many things to keep track of!*

As Kamala shrugged on her jacket at the end of the school day, she made a decision. There would be no crime-fighting tonight. Nothing was going to distract her from studying.

Kamala texted Nakia as she walked home from school.

Nakia
Last-minute study date tomorrow night?
I need you to whip me into shape for this big test.
Sure! Where?
Your place?
Sounds good! Get ready to have your butt kicked.

"Pardon me," a deep voice boomed. Kamala looked up. The largest homeless person she had ever seen was standing in front of her. His tattered hat hid his hair and his long, stained coat hid the rest of him, but there was still something kind of familiar about him.

SORRY.
I DON'T HAVE ANY CHANGE.

She kept walking. The man walked with her.

"I do not seek money," he said in that booming voice. **"I seek you. You must come with me, Ms. Marvel."**

Kamala stopped short. He knew who she was, and he was obviously looking for trouble. This wasn't good.

"I must, huh?" Kamala said, her hands on her hips, glaring up at the guy.

Whoever this guy was, he could get lost. Kamala was going to study tonight, not get into a fight with yet another weirdo.

"Do you not wish to protect yourself?" the man asked.

Was he threatening her? He was! How dare he? All the stresses of the day suddenly piled up on her.

It just wasn't FAIR.

"Okay," Kamala said furiously. "That's it. Let's go." This guy was going to get it.

"Excellent," the man said cheerfully. **"I shall lead the way!"** He started walking away, clearly expecting her to follow him.

"No, *I* shall," Kamala said, and walked into an empty alley. She didn't want people to see ordinary teenager Kamala Khan kicking this giant guy's butt. But she didn't have time to change out of her normal clothes. Luckily, the alley was deserted.

"What a fine alleyway," the man remarked pleasantly as he followed her, looking around. **"But I fail to—OOMPH!"** He grunted in surprise as Kamala punched him in the stomach.

Kamala's knuckles throbbed painfully. Hitting

this guy was like punching a brick wall.

"Okay," Kamala said, trying to shake out her hand without looking like a big dork. Luckily, her accelerated healing meant that her hand would be fine in no time.

Kamala kicked and punched, using every bit

of training she had. She embiggened to the size of a car. She shrank down to the size of a cat. She was a flurry of motion, her fists flying. But soon she started to feel pretty foolish, because the big guy didn't seem to feel her blows at all. In fact, he wasn't even fighting back.

He was just standing there, saying things like **"Wait!"** and **"Perhaps I could have been clearer."**

"You were plenty clear when you *threatened me*!" Kamala snapped, doing her best to give the guy a black eye. But he ducked under her fist, and she knocked off his hat instead. Kamala grabbed him by the front of his coat to swing him around, but the threadbare fabric tore right down the back seam. The man's hat and coat hit the ground.

Kamala gasped and stepped back. Standing in front of her, was

THE MIGHTY THOR

It was really Thor. Not a villain. But then why had he threatened her?

Thinking back on what he actually said, Kamala realized suddenly that he had been *warning* her.

This is the worst, she thought. *I just tried to beat up Thor. I just tried to beat up an Avenger!*

"Forgive me if I was unclear," Thor said. **"Perhaps I should introduce myself."**

"I know who you are. I have, like, four action figures of you in my room," Kamala blurted out.

Way to go, Kamala. Real cool.

She made a fist and tapped it against her forehead. A little too hard. Then she gave an awkward smile. "Ah-ha-ha. I mean . . . um. Never mind."

"I call this one Tiny Thor," Kamala said, making the little action figure do a funny dance. She picked up another one. "And this is Fashion Thor. I stole the butterfly hair clips from Nakia when we were, like, five years old."

"Very fierce," Thor said seriously. He picked up another action figure of himself and examined it carefully. Kamala shook her head. *Thor the Avenger* was sitting on her bedroom floor, rummaging through a bin of old toys with her, asking her about her collection of . . . well, *him*. It was one of the weirdest things that had happened to her since she became a Super Hero. And that was really saying something.

"That's Peg Leg Thor," Kamala said. "He lost his leg, so I had to replace it with a clothespin."

"How careless of him," Thor said, frowning down at the one-legged action figure disapprovingly. Kamala leaped to his defense. "Not careless—brave!" she said. "He lost it in battle! It was a valiant struggle. Against a *Tyrannosaurus rex*."

She dug the plastic T. rex out of the bin of toys. "See?" Kamala said, showing Thor. "A formidable opponent."

"With an honorable wound to match," Thor said, satisfied. **"Kamala, I apologize for approaching you in disguise. I was trying to 'keep a low profile,' as Hawkeye puts it."**

"Don't worry about it," Kamala said. "It's not your fault—I'm just super on edge lately. I've got a lot on my plate. Sorry I overreacted."

"You are forgiven," Thor said.

She was feeling a little starstruck. She had even more action figures of Hawkeye than of Thor. But she didn't want to hurt Thor's feelings, so she didn't tell him that.

"I have come to your city to investigate a string of pet-store robberies that have been committed over the last several months," Thor said.

"Yikes," Kamala said. "That's pretty weird. What are they stealing? Tell me it isn't puppies."

"Birds," Thor said, **"and many of them."**

"Huh," Kamala said. "You know, the girl who was trying to rob that pet store this morning was wearing some kind of dumb bird mask. And she was making bird noises, too."

"Yes," Thor said. **"The intelligence that we have received at Avengers Headquarters has been . . ."**

"Disturbing?" Kamala suggested.

"Silly," Thor finished.

Kamala nodded in agreement.

"Regardless," Thor continued, **"I have been sent to investigate. I was not planning to include you in the investigation, even though Jersey City is your 'turf,' as Hawkeye puts it. I did not want to endanger you, because you are so young."**

"I can handle myself!" Kamala protested.

"Yes," Thor said, **"I learned that today. In any case, I overheard several of these teenage**

bird-people discussing their plan to target you, Ms. Marvel. And I realized I must warn you."

"So what's next?" Kamala asked, trying to act cool—like hearing Thor himself call her by her Super Hero name wasn't the best thing that had ever happened to her.

"Obviously you must stay safely indoors while I conduct my investigation," Thor said.

Kamala frowned. "Normally I try to at least pretend to obey authority figures. You know, people like my imam. Or ancient alien Super Heroes like you."

"Very wise," Thor agreed.

"But come on," Kamala continued. "This is *Jersey*. Hawkeye was right—this *is* my turf. If you don't let me team up with you, I'm going to do my own investigation anyway, and then we'll just get in each other's way. You don't want to be tripping over me every time you turn around, right?"

Thor frowned. **"It would indeed be more efficient to work together,"** he said reluctantly.

From downstairs, Kamala heard her father's voice. "Kamala? Who are you talking to? Is there someone in your room?"

Kamala jumped. "You have to get out of here!" she told Thor. "Quick!"

"Kamala?" her father called again.

"Who is in there with you?"

"Out the window!" Kamala hissed, waving her arms frantically at Thor. "I'll meet you later!"

In the hallway outside his daughter's room, Yusuf Khan paused to listen. The murmur of voices had stopped. There was a strange *whoosh*, and then silence again. But Yusuf was certain he'd heard another voice inside the room. He knocked on Kamala's door and opened it.

"What on earth is going on in here?" Yusuf said, looking around. But the only person in the room was his daughter. She was sitting on the floor, surrounded by plastic toys. In one hand Kamala was holding a small plastic man with a red cape. In the other, she was holding a houseplant in a clay pot.

"Oh, hi, Abu," she said, smiling.

"I thought I heard voices," Yusuf said, looking around in confusion.

"Nobody here but me and Thor," Kamala said. She waved the small plastic toy, and its little red cape fluttered. "He's fighting crime with a new partner."

Kamala turned back to her game. She waggled the toy as though it was talking to the plant. **"IT IS I, THOR!"** Kamala said in a booming, deep voice. **"COME, THOU POTTED VEGETATION. THOU AND I MUST HIE UNTO ASGARD ANON. FORSOOTH AND GADZOOKS!"**

Yusuf shook his head and smiled. It was nice to be reminded every now and then that Kamala was still his goofy little girl.

He shut the door behind him and went back downstairs to finish reading the newspaper.

CHAPTER 4

That afternoon, Kamala tried—and failed—to study for her test.

"Come on," she told herself, squinting at her Biology textbook. "You aren't meeting Thor until tonight. You have three hours of primo study time. You can do this. You *have* to do this."

She gripped her highlighter tight and started reading. But the words ran together on the page. Kamala stared blankly down at the book while her mind raced over the mystery of the pet-shop

burglaries. Why were these bird-people stealing from pet shops? What were they after? And why was this happening in New Jersey? In Ms. Marvel's territory?

Come to think, why were they talking about going after Ms. Marvel in the first place?

Finally, Kamala threw down her highlighter in frustration and instead opened a web browser on her computer.

If I can't get any studying done, she thought,

I might as well do something *productive.*

Soon, Kamala was deep in a search through local news sites, looking for any information about the pet-shop robberies.

She clicked through to an article about a break-in at the PUPPY PILE, a pet store in Edison, NJ.

Break-In at the Puppy Pile
"They didn't even take any money," said Anita Batra, the owner of the Puppy Pile. "That was the weirdest thing. The cash register was right there, but instead they went straight to the birdcages at

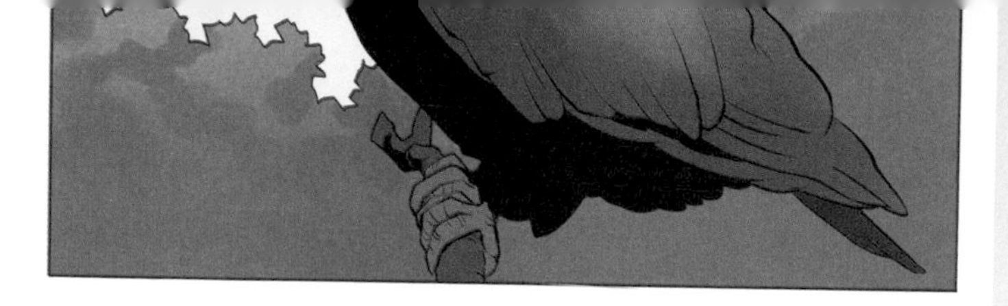

Break-In at the Puppy Pile

"They didn't even take any money," said Anita Batra, the owner of the Puppy Pile. "That was the weirdest thing. The cash register was right there, but instead they went straight to the birdcages at the back of the store."

The criminals made off with seven canaries and an African grey parrot. They are described as three teenagers wearing bird costumes.

"I'm pretty sure one of them was levitating," said Ms. Batra. Police are investigating the robbery and have released a statement saying that the suspects are thought to have superhuman abilities of some kind.

Meanwhile, the Puppy Pile is planning to reopen on Monday, but Ms. Batra says she still hopes the police find her missing birds soon

That night, after bedtime, Kamala stuffed a pillow under the covers. She hoped it looked like she was still in bed, asleep. Then she changed into her her "sneaking around" clothes, grabbed her backpack, and embiggened her legs until they were long enough to reach the ground outside. She stepped quietly out of her second-story window.

Kamala shrank her legs back down and looked around. Sure enough—Thor was standing in the shadows under a tree. He waved at her and Kamala trotted over, being careful to make no noise. The last thing she needed was to wake up her parents.

"Hail and well met, my sister in arms!" Thor boomed out as she reached him.

"Shush!!!" Kamala said, waving her hands desperately at him. Then she panicked for a whole different reason.

Thor was an *Avenger* and she'd just told him to *shush*?

"I mean," she said, backpedaling, "I'm sorry, but if you wouldn't mind—"

Thor shook his head. **"No apologies are needed, except from me. I admit I am not accustomed to stealth."**

"I can tell. You wore the cape and everything," Kamala said, relieved. "But let's get out of here, yeah?"

"Yeah!" said Thor. **"I mean, yeah."**

Thor wanted to see the pet store where Kamala had foiled the latest robbery, that morning. So they went there first, and Kamala showed Thor the scene of the crime.

"I was standing out here," she said. "The robber was in the back of the store."

Thor peered through the window into the darkened store. **"What manner of animals are kept in the back?"** he asked.

"Not sure," Kamala said. She pulled out her flashlight. "Let's see."

The bright circle of light glinted off a row of birdcages in the back of the store.

"Birds again," Kamala said thoughtfully. She explained to Thor about the article she'd read earlier. "So they're stealing birds, wearing bird masks, and making sounds like birds . . . what else do we know?

"At least some of the suspects have supernatural abilities, perhaps all of them."

"Superpowered bird fans stealing birds," Kamala said. Then something occurred to her. "Hey, there's a pet store right here in Jersey City that *only* sells birds. It's called BETSY'S BITSY BIRDIES. Do you know if it's been robbed, too?"

"Not yet," Thor said. **"But perhaps . . ."**

"Just in case . . ." Ms. Marvel agreed. She looked up the address on her phone, and they were off.

Kamala and Thor arrived at Betsy's Bitsy Birdies ten minutes later. The store was dark and quiet. All the windows were unbroken, and the door was closed.

Kamala and Thor climbed into a tree and hid quietly. Sure enough, not long after that, a group of teenagers wearing bird masks came sneaking up to Betsy's Bitsy Birdies.

"This is the place," one of them said.

"Jackpot!" said another. "We're going to be

his favorites after we come back with all these birds."

A third birdlike teen raised her arm. She was gripping a brick. Just as she was about to smash it through the window, Kamala shot her elongated arm out and grabbed her.

"Squawk!" yelled the teen.

"Squawk! Squawk!" yelled her friends, trying to tug her out of Kamala's grip. But it was too late. Hanging from his flying hammer, Thor glided out of the tree and straight into the fray. He kicked the two teens away from their friend and got to work tying them up.

"This young woman seems to have super strength," Thor remarked. He grunted as he struggled to subdue the girl. **"Luckily, my ropes are magic bindings from the halls of Asgard."**

The girl chirped sullenly as Thor tied a firm knot around her wrists.

"Okay," Kamala said once the three teenage burglars were all tied up. "I've called the cops. Now talk. Why are you stealing birds? Who do you work for?"

The three teens stared at Kamala and Thor in silence.

"Wait," Kamala said, "are your masks made of real feathers?"

"Peep," the superstrong girl said, glaring defiantly at Ms. Marvel.

Thor reached out and plucked a feather from her head.

"Peep!"

CHAPTER 5

After the police arrived, Kamala and Thor went to a twenty-four-hour shawarma place for a post-crime-fighting midnight snack. Kamala was famished, so she ate two whole sandwiches. Thor ate seven.

"Is your friend okay?" the waitress asked Kamala. "That's just . . . a lot of shawarma."

Thor burped delicately into a napkin. **"Delicious. I'll have another,"** he said. **"This time, extra sauce. And extra bread. And meat. Actually I'll just have two more sandwiches."**

"Are you sure?" the waitress asked, still looking a little worried. "Maybe you should take a breather. The shawarma isn't going anywhere."

"It's okay," Kamala said reassuringly. "He's from Asgard. They probably eat, like, whole turkeys for dinner there."

"Once I ate two oxen," Thor said proudly. **"They still tell the tale to this day."**

"See?" Kamala said.

All told, Kamala wasn't in bed until 2:00 a.m. She woke up the next morning more tired than she'd been when she went to bed. The only thing that kept her awake during her classes was the memory of those three bird-people, with their weirdly elaborate masks.

What is this all about? Kamala thought for the millionth time as she stumbled down the school steps at the end of the day.

"Kamala!" a familiar voice boomed out. It was Thor, back in his homeless-person disguise.

"You know," she said, walking up to him, "even in disguise, you're super obvious."

Thor frowned. **"Perhaps I should have a different disguise, but I have more urgent business to share with you right now."**

Kamala followed Thor into the alleyway where they had first fought. "What's up?"

"I have been to Asgard," Thor said, holding up the feather he'd plucked off the bird-girl's head the night before. **"I had our best alchemists examine this feather, to determine its origin."**

Kamala looked up from where she was stashing her civilian clothing behind the Dumpster. "And?" she asked.

"The girl is an Inhuman," Thor said. **"With bird DNA in her genome."**

Kamala's eyes widened. "So those weren't masks? You're telling me those kids are Inhuman. Like me? Except not quite like me. I don't have bird . . . stuff."

"Avian genetic material," Thor filled in.

"Exactly," Kamala said. "And these kids are working for someone. Someone with a plan. But who?"

Thor furrowed his brow. **"It would have to be a great mastermind,"** he said. **"And someone familiar with New Jersey."**

"And someone with a grudge against me," Kamala said.

"And someone with an interest in birds," Thor added.

Kamala gasped. "I have an idea! But it's impossible. The only person I can think of who fits this description is . . . No, it couldn't be!"

"Who?" Thor asked.

"The Inventor," Kamala said, referring to the bird-man Super Villain she had defeated early in her career. "He hates me, and he's half bird himself. But he's in prison!"

Kamala pulled out her phone and entered a search in the web browser. "At least he *was* in prison . . ." she murmured as she tapped through to a recent article.

Despite concerted effort
by local law enforcement
there is still no sign of the
Inventor, New Jersey's own
birdlike Super Villain, who
escaped from prison several
months ago. Authorities have
redoubled efforts to locate
this avian menace,
but several leads have

Despite concerted effort by local law enforcement there is still no sign of the Inventor, New Jersey's own birdlike Super Villain, who escaped from prison several months ago. Authorities have redoubled efforts to locate this avian menace, but several leads

"Oops," Kamala said.

"So we have our slime suspect," Thor said. **"The Inventor."**

"I think you mean '*prime* suspect,'" Kamala said.

"I am quite sure Hawkeye said the term was 'slime suspect,'" Thor protested.

Kamala tried not to laugh.

Later that night, Kamala and Thor sneaked through a chain-link fence in an industrial park. "The police haven't found the Inventor but they don't know him the way I do. He loves these spooky abandoned plants."

"You seem very confident," Thor remarked.

"Well," Kamala said. "I kind of do the Super Hero thing a lot. But you do, too, I guess."

"Indeed," Thor said. **"I think perhaps you and I have more in common than I would have thought."**

"What do you mean?" Kamala asked. She pulled out Bruno's custom lock-zapper—a handy

gadget he'd made just for her—and pointed it at the side door to the plant. Then a little light flashed red and the door made an alarming **CRUNCH** sound.

Kamala tried the doorknob, but it wouldn't turn. She frowned. "Stupid gadget," she muttered at it. "Be more open-y." She zapped the lock again, and this time it **CRUNCHED** even more loudly. A seam of melted metal appeared around the edge of the door. The door was now firmly welded to the door frame.

"ARGH!" Kamala yelled. **"WHAT IS WRONG WITH THIS THING?"**

"I believe you hit the wrong button," Thor said. Kamala looked at the device again. Sure enough, it had two buttons.

Kamala buried her face in her hands. She felt so stupid—for hitting the wrong button, but also for getting so mad about it.

Thor cleared his throat delicately. **"Allow me,"** he said. With a gentle tug, he wrenched the door *and* the door frame right out of the wall.

"As I was saying," Thor continued, **"we have much in common, you and I. For example, we both like to celebrate a hard-won battle with a mighty feast."**

Kamala nodded. "That was some good shawarma last night," she said. "I always get super hungry after a fight."

"As do I," said Thor. **"And then of course—ahem—our short tempers."**

Kamala was quiet. She looked around the empty plant. "Nothing here."

As they trudged out of the plant, she shook her head thoughtfully. "You're right about my short temper," she said after a while. "But it's worse than usual, these days."

"Why?" Thor asked, swinging his hammer into the sky. Kamala grabbed his arm and they sailed into the air.

"Head due north," she instructed him. Then, in answer to his question: "Oh, I don't know. I guess I've just got a lot to deal with lately. School, friends, family, and then this Super Hero-ing thing. I worry that it's changing me. It's making me . . . *mean*."

Thor was silent, but it was an understanding kind of silence. Kamala stared down at the dark industrial wastelands beneath them and sighed.

"Sometimes I don't know how long I can keep doing this."

CHAPTER 6

Kamala and Thor investigated six abandoned plants before they finally found one with a light glimmering dimly in one of its broken windows.

"This has *got* to be him," Kamala whispered, as they landed in the courtyard outside the plant. Thor nodded. He tilted his head, listening.

"I hear voices," he said. **"Many voices. If this is truly the Inventor's stronghold, he has others defending it with him."**

Kamala shook her head to clear it. It was nearly 4:00 a.m., and she was so tired. "If it's more of those birdlike Inhumans, I can probably take a few of them at once," she said. Then she yawned so widely it felt like her jaw was going to fall off.

Thor smiled. **"I do not think you could take on a stiff breeze right now,"** he said gently. **"He will still be here tomorrow. Let us get you home."**

"But I—" Kamala said, cutting herself off with another yawn.

"You are in no shape for a showdown," Thor said. He put his arm around her waist and swung his hammer up. **"Let's get you to bed."**

Kamala nodded sleepily as they rocketed into the sky. "Okay," she said. "Bed."

Kamala Khan woke up feeling like death warmed over. She squinted blearily at her alarm clock, which was bleeping at her. 7:00 a.m. Time to get up. Time to eat breakfast. Time to go to school. Time to take that big Biology test.

Kamala sat bolt upright, her heart hammering in her chest.

"THE TEST!" she yelled. She had forgotten all about the big Biology test. She hadn't even studied—

"NAKIA!" she yelled even louder.

She'd blown off her study date the night before with Nakia!

"Oh my glob," she moaned. "I'm going to fail the test, *and* Nakia is never going to forgive me."

Kamala was almost afraid to go to her locker that morning. And sure enough, there was Nakia, adjusting her hijab in front of her mirror. When she saw Kamala approaching, Nakia shut her locker and turned.

"Nakia, I'm **SO** sorry—" Kamala started.

"I texted you twenty-two times," Nakia said.

"I know," Kamala moaned. She'd seen the texts when she finally checked her phone, on the way to school that morning.

"*Where were you?*" Nakia asked.

"I . . ." Kamala shook her head. "I don't want to lie to you. But I can't tell you that."

“I don’t even want to see your face right now,” Nakia said. She turned and walked into the Biology classroom. Numbly, Kamala followed her.

Kamala made it halfway through the Biology test before she just gave up.

“May I go to the bathroom?” she asked, raising her hand.

“Not during a test,” Mr. Lukoff said.

“I’m done,” Kamala said. She handed the half-filled-out test to Mr. Lukoff and left the room.

Kamala managed to keep it together until she got to the girls' bathroom. Tears began to stream down her face and she punched the tiled wall.

Kamala was so angry

she could hardly think.

Everything was falling apart,

and it was all the

INVENTOR'S

FAULT!

CHAPTER 7

Kamala didn't wait for Thor. As soon as school was out, she changed into her Ms. Marvel costume in her usual alley and started walking.

As she went, she **elongated** her legs until each stride was a block long.

Soon, Ms. Marvel was outside the Jersey City limits. And not long after that, she was sloshing through the marshes of industrial New Jersey. Normally she would have been grossed out by the squishy mud of the marshland, but today she was too angry to even notice.

This is the Inventor's fault. My life is a mess, and it's his fault. I failed the test, and it's his fault. My best friend hates me, and it's his fault.

Ms. Marvel was ready to fight. In fact, she couldn't wait. The Inventor was going to pay.

Soon the Inventor's lair was in sight. But before Ms. Marvel reached the fence, an Inhuman teenager stepped out of the tall grass and stood in her way.

Ba-GRACK!

"Stop right there," he sneered. **"Ba-GRACK!"** He raked one foot through the dirt, and Ms. Marvel saw that instead of human feet he had long, scaly claws like a rooster. He was different from the other bird-people she'd seen so far—he even had a wattle, like a chicken. He looked ridiculous.

Ba-CRAWK!

Ms. Marvel rolled her eyes. "Get out of my way."

"No can do, Ms. Moron," the boy said, dodging back into her path.

"Very funny," Ms. Marvel said.

"It's funny because Moron and Marvel both start with the letter *M*," the kid said. "Basically, I just called you stupid."

"Yep," Ms. Marvel said, pushing the boy out of her way.

"But in a funny, clever way," the boy added, pecking at her. **"Ba-CRAWK!"**

"Nope," Ms. Marvel said, batting him away. "Not funny, not clever. Now scram."

"Too bad!" the chicken-boy said. "The Inventor and everyone else aren't even at headquarters right now. He left me here to guard the place all by myself until he gets back. **Gra-KACK!"**

"Great," Ms. Marvel said grimly. "Then I'll just wait for him there, shall I?"

She tried once more to push the boy aside and keep walking toward the plant. But the chicken-boy danced around her, pecking at her arms with his weird beak-nose and scratching at her with his taloned feet. Ms. Marvel couldn't take a step without tripping over him.

"*Get out of my way!*" she finally yelled, at the end of her rope.

"Ca-BAWK! Make me!" jeered the chicken-boy. "Try and make me, Ms. Moron! Ha-ha-ha! Ms. Moron! Ms. Moron! Ms.—"

CRACK!

Ms. Marvel punched the chicken-boy as hard as she could. She hit him so hard that her whole arm tingled. For a moment, it felt good. It felt satisfying. But then as she watched him stagger back, it stopped feeling good. His eyes were wide and shocked, and his mouth was bloody. Ms. Marvel had hit him harder than she needed to . . . a lot harder. He was really hurt.

The chicken-boy abruptly sat down on the ground and started crying. He was holding his face, but Ms. Marvel could tell she'd knocked out at least one of his teeth. She'd been in enough fights to know what that looked like. And this boy was younger than she was—he couldn't have been older than fourteen.

Ms. Marvel felt like a complete monster.

"Oh no," she said. "I'm so sorry." She rushed over to the boy, but he recoiled, scooting away from her.

"Don't touch me!" he said, the words muffled. "It hurts!" Tears were sliding down his face, and suddenly he wasn't annoying anymore . . . he was just pathetic.

"Oh man," Ms. Marvel said. She got out her phone and dialed 9-1-1. The boy continued to cry as she gave their location to the police.

"An ambulance is coming. You're going to be okay."

"I wuh-wuh-want my mommmmmm," the boy sobbed.

"Okay," Ms. Marvel said, feeling lower than low. "We'll call her, too." She sat down next to the boy and handed him her phone.

"You're mean," he muttered as he dialed.

"Yeah," Ms. Marvel said grimly. "I think you might be right."

Ms. Marvel stayed with the chicken-boy until the ambulance arrived and took him away. Then

she sat by herself on the ground, staring into space for a long time afterward.

The chicken-boy had been harmless. Annoying, sure, but harmless. Ms. Marvel was a hero—or she was supposed to be one, anyway.

"I'm supposed to be better than this," she said softly to herself. "I'm supposed to be the good guy."

But she'd been so angry at the Inventor for messing up her week that she'd let herself really hurt someone who wasn't anywhere near as strong as she was.

She'd failed her Biology test, she'd failed her friend, and she'd failed as a hero.

"I don't deserve to be called Ms. Marvel," Kamala Khan said softly, pulling her mask off and burying her face in her hands.

CHAPTER 8

Thor found her there, letting her mind spin around in circles of anger and self-blame.

He had to wave his hand in front of Kamala's face a few times before she noticed him.

"Oh," she said, "it's you."

"Should not you be wearing your mask, Ms. Marvel?" Thor asked gently, crouching down in front of her. He picked her mask up off the ground and offered it to her.

Kamala stared at it blankly for a while and then shook her head.

"I'm not feeling very heroic," she said. She told Thor all about what had happened.

"I thought it was the Inventor's fault that my life is a mess," Kamala finished, "but it's my fault. I'm the one who forgot to study for the test.

I'm the one who let down my friend. I'm the one who's messing things up every day. I just didn't want to face it, and I took it out on that stupid chicken kid."

Thor sat down next to her and stared thoughtfully up at the sky.

"Perhaps you do not believe this," he said, **"but I have felt the same way myself."**

Kamala squinted at him skeptically. "You're right," she said. "I don't believe it."

Thor sighed. **"I was not always as wise or as humble as I am now,"** he said. **"When I was a younger man, I had many faults. I was arrogant. I was impatient."**

He paused. **"To be fair,"** he said, **"I *was* very handsome, brave, and fierce in battle. I still am!"**

Kamala smiled and poked Thor in the side. "And wise and humble, too."

Thor grinned. **"Perhaps not *perfectly* humble,"** he admitted. **"We are none of us perfect."**

"No," Kamala said sadly. "We aren't. Me especially."

"But that is my point," Thor said. **"Heed my tale, Kamala Khan. There came a day when I realized that I was nothing more than an arrogant child. And on that day, I doubted."**

Kamala looked up at him. Thor was still staring at the sky, but there was something in his face that she recognized, because it was the same thing she was feeling.

"I doubted myself," Thor continued. **"I saw that I had been vain, cruel, and thoughtless.** ***This man is no hero,*** **I thought.** ***This man is a fool."***

Kamala's heart twisted a little in her chest. "What did you do?" she asked.

"I learned to accept two important things," Thor said. **"First, that I was not perfect. Then, that I did not need to be, as long as I kept trying."**

Kamala frowned. "I know you're hoping to make me feel better about how badly I screwed up," she said, "but I don't buy it. You seem pretty perfect to me. You're an *Avenger.*"

"I am an Avenger because I have learned to accept my faults," Thor said. **"And if I were perfect, I would have realized immediately that 'slime suspect' is not a thing."**

Kamala giggled. "See, Hawkeye knows what being an Avenger is *really* all about," she said. "Pranking your teammates."

"Indeed," Thor said, smiling. Then he looked at Kamala very seriously. **"You have failed today, but that does not mean you are a failure. You cannot do everything perfectly, Kamala Khan, and you cannot do everything by yourself."**

Kamala smiled. "Thank you, Thor," she said. "That means a lot to me." And she really did feel better. There was something amazing about knowing that **THOR, THE MIGHTY AVENGER,** had once dealt with the same doubts and fears.

"There is no need to thank me," Thor said. He handed Kamala her Ms. Marvel mask again, and this time she accepted it. **"And you should not be so hard on yourself. You are a better person at sixteen than I was at nine hundred."**

"Aw," Kamala said, throwing her arms around Thor, "you don't look a day over eight hundred and ninety-nine."

Evening was dimming into night when Ms. Marvel and Thor approached the Inventor's lair at last. "I think he must be back by now," Ms. Marvel said. "Hopefully we've still got the drop on him."

Then a shout shattered the quiet night air.

"It's time!" A shrill, unpleasant voice erupted from the factory tower. **"My brilliance knows no bounds!"**

Ms. Marvel and Thor looked at each other.

"That's definitely the Inventor's voice," Ms. Marvel said.

"Tonight, we take Jersey City," the Inventor yelled. **"And tomorrow—"**

"Ah, I know this one," Thor told Kamala. He threw a fist into the air as though he were a maniacal villain. **"And tomorrow, the world!"** he said, mimicking the Inventor.

"The world?" Ms. Marvel replied incredulously. "With *that* gang of birdbrains as his army?"

"And tomorrow, the New York metropolitan area!" the Inventor finished triumphantly from inside the factory.

"That seems more reasonable," Thor remarked.

"And shortly after that," the Inventor added, still yelling, **"the tristate area! And then, following our takeover of the northeastern**

United States, we'll move on to the Eastern Seaboard—"

"Should we just go in right now?" Ms. Marvel said. "I feel like this could go on for a while."

"By all means," Thor said. He offered his arm, and Ms. Marvel grabbed it. Thor swung Mjolnir skyward, and the two heroes sailed into the sky, heading directly toward the tower.

IT WAS TIME TO FIGHT.

CHAPTER 9

Deep in the New Jersey marshlands, the Secaucus Amalgamated Macaroni Company's pasta manufacturing plant had stood empty for decades before the Inventor moved his latest sinister operation into it. But now it was full of activity. Empty birdcages hung from the rafters, and the Inventor's henchmen—both bird-people and robots—patrolled the corridors. And in the tower, a giant contraption stood, crackling with electrical sparks.

Thor and Ms. Marvel had just enough time to take in the scene below them before they crashed through the skylight in the tower and landed amid a small army of birdlike teenage Inhumans.

A siren blared. Ms. Marvel and Thor stood up, brushing broken glass off themselves.

"**Get 'em!**" squawked one of the Inventor's Inhuman henchmen. And with a flurry of feathers and a chorus of cheeps, they attacked.

Ba-GRACK!
Squawk!
Ba-CRAWK!
Squawk!

Ms. Marvel embiggened her fists, **lengthened** her arms, and threw herself into the fight. The first Inhuman to attack her clawed at Ms. Marvel's face, but Ms. Marvel grabbed her by the tail and tossed her into a pile of old boxes.

Nearby, Thor was fighting off seven fluffy Inhumans covered in downy yellow feathers. They were all making high-pitched peeps. **"I do not wish to harm you!"** Thor yelled at the duckling-like villains. **"For you are extremely adorable! Ouch!"** he added as one of them bit him.

Ms. Marvel started in Thor's direction to help him, but she was suddenly knocked sideways by a robot hurtling out of a dark corner. The Inventor's robots were dangerous—Ms. Marvel had fought them before. She picked herself up and jumped sideways, dodging a laser blast.

"Yaaah!" Ms. Marvel yelled, using her embiggened fist to smash the robot to pieces.

Ms. Marvel took a deep breath, hoping for a little break so she could help out Thor. But just then, three more bird-people and another laser-armed robot all charged her at once. In a blur of fists and feet, Ms. Marvel kicked and punched—swung and spun—until she was surrounded by the scraps of the robot, and all her attackers were tied up. Her lungs were heaving and her fists were aching.

"I don't know how many more of them I can handle," Ms. Marvel said to Thor.

"How about one more?" said a sneering, shrill voice.

Ms. Marvel looked up. Standing in front of the giant machine was the Inventor. He was dramatically silhouetted against the sparking waves of electricity.

"I bid you welcome," he said, **"to your *doom.*"**

"At least he is polite," Thor remarked, smashing the robot onto the cement floor.

The Inventor snapped his fingers, and the rest of the robots and Inhumans backed away from Ms. Marvel and Thor.

"Perhaps you're wondering what I am doing here," the Inventor said, strolling slowly toward them. **"Well, make yourselves comfortable, and**

I shall tell you a tale the likes of which—"

"You're stealing pet birds and putting their DNA into Inhuman teenagers you recruited for your villainous army of superpowered bird-people," Ms. Marvel said.

"Oh," the Inventor said, annoyed. **"Yes, well. Got it in one."**

"Cool," Ms. Marvel said. She embiggened until she was nearly as high as the ceiling. "How about we move straight to the final-showdown part of the evening?"

"You don't want to hear more about my revolutionary new nuclease enzyme? It's perfect for gene-splicing!"

"I'd really rather fight," Ms. Marvel admitted. "And besides, Biology is sort of a sore subject for me right now."

"If you insist," the Inventor said and snapped his fingers. Suddenly a huge robot loomed up behind him—it was easily as big as all of the other robots put together.

Ms. Marvel's heart sank. She'd never taken on a robot this big.

I don't think I can do this, she thought.

But then she remembered what Thor had told her. *You cannot do everything by yourself.*

With help, though, she could do pretty much anything.

"Let's go!" Ms. Marvel yelled, and she and Thor leaped into action. Thor drew the laser fire away from Ms. Marvel by flying up to the ceiling and zigzagging across the room. Meanwhile, Ms. Marvel smashed at the robot's legs with her embiggened fists. Now the robot had noticed her. It stopped shooting lasers at Thor and started shooting them at Ms. Marvel instead!

Ms. Marvel leaped out of the way just a little too slowly. One of the lasers hit her on the arm.

"AUGH!" she screamed, rolling behind a big cement column. She looked at her arm. It was bleeding a little, and it hurt terribly.

Taking a deep breath, Ms. Marvel dived out from behind the column. **She had to help!**

Frantically looking around the old factory, Ms. Marvel spotted a huge, dusty old piece of equipment. It said ***MACARONI MASTER 3000*** on the side, and it looked like it weighed about a ton. Ms. Marvel embiggened herself until she was big enough to pick up the macaroni press. Then she heaved it up into the air and bashed it hard against the robot.

There was a terrible grinding noise, as the robot shuddered and ground to a halt. The lights along its body dimmed down and finally winked out.

CRUNCH!

"We did it!" Ms. Marvel cried. She turned to Thor. "High five!" she said, holding up her hand.

"Ah!" Thor said. **"I know this one. Hawkeye taught me."** He high-fived her back. **"Did I do it right?"** he asked.

"Yep!" Ms. Marvel said. She looked around. All the fight seemed to have gone out of the Inventor's birdlike henchmen. The few that Ms. Marvel and Thor hadn't already defeated were sitting down, muttering unhappily. "We give up!" one said. "Please don't tell our parents! We just signed on because we were bored!"

"I wasn't bored," another Inhuman teen said. "I just did it so I'd have something to write my college application essays about."

"I did it on a dare," said another birdlike henchman.

"I did it because all my friends were doing it," said a girl with purple feathers.

Ms. Marvel rolled her eyes. She was about to launch into an angry lecture about how dumb it was to sign on with a villain like the Inventor for *any* reason, when she realized . . .

"Where *is* the Inventor?"

Ms. Marvel looked around the factory, and a sudden motion caught her eye. It was the Inventor, running for the door!

Quick as lightning, Ms. Marvel stretched her arms out and caught the Inventor.

"Not so fast!" she said. "You've got to pay for your crimes. Also, you have to help untangle this mess." She pointed at the sullen teenagers sitting around the factory. "What happened to all the birds you used, anyway?"

"I'll never tell!" the Inventor shrieked. **"My twisted creations will be stuck like that forever! Ha-ha-ha-ha-ha!"**

"It's this button, isn't it?" Thor said, pointing at a big red button on the mysterious machine.

"**No?**" the Inventor said unconvincingly.

"That's a yes," Ms. Marvel said. Thor pushed the button, and there was a huge **CRACKLE** as electricity coursed through the machine.

After a few seconds, Ms. Marvel blinked stars out of her eyes and looked around.

All the birdlike teenagers were now just normal teenagers. And the factory was full of exotic birds flying in confused circles.

CHAPTER 10

It took most of the night for the police to cart away the Inventor and all his juvenile sidekicks, and even longer for a local animal rescue to come collect all the pet birds. By the time the cleanup was done, even Thor looked a little worn-out.

"Shawarma?" he said hopefully.

"I was hoping you'd say that," Ms. Marvel said with a grin.

Soon the two Super Heroes were sitting in their usual corner of the all-night shawarma shop in Jersey City. Thor ordered seven sandwiches again, but the waitress brought him ten.

"On the house," she said. "Mostly I just want to see if you can actually eat ten of these."

"Good lady, I will endeavor not to disappoint," Thor said grandly and dug in.

He was halfway through the fifth sandwich when the door opened with a cheerful little chime, and Hawkeye walked in.

Ms. Marvel almost choked on her sandwich.

What was Hawkeye doing at Nour's Kebab Hut at two in the morning?

"Yo, Thor," he said, plopping into the booth at their table. "What's up, Ms. Marvel?"

Ms. Marvel managed a muffled "Hi" around her half-chewed bite of shawarma.

"Well met, my friend!" Thor boomed, clapping Hawkeye on the shoulder so hard he nearly fell out of his chair. **"Have you come to sample Nour's wares? Truly, her sandwiches are the best in Jersey City."**

"No," Hawkeye said, "I'm here because the Avengers are assembling. If you're done with your investigation here in

New Jersey, we need you back at HQ. It's kind of an emergency."

Thor stuffed the rest of his sandwich into his mouth, nodding vigorously. He stood up and grabbed Mjolnir.

"Hey!" the waitress said, coming out from the kitchen. "You did it! You ate five sandwiches!"

Thor grinned widely, his cheeks stuffed full of shawarma, and held up his hand for a celebratory high five. The waitress slapped his palm.

"You know who taught him to high-five?" Hawkeye asked Ms. Marvel quietly.

"It's a mystery, and you're the slime suspect," Ms. Marvel shot back, deadpan.

Hawkeye gave her a wide-eyed, innocent stare. "I have absolutely no idea what you're talking about," he said, softly enough that Thor, who was still talking to the waitress, couldn't hear. "I would never prank another Avenger like that. For instance, I definitely have not replaced Thor's conditioner with glue."

Kamala giggled and then turned to Thor. She wrapped her arms around his gigantic body. Thor hugged her back.

"Truly it has been an honor fighting at your side, my mighty

friend," he said. **"Remember: there is great honor in accepting help."**

"Thanks, Thor," Ms. Marvel said. "And here is some wisdom from me to you: throw away your conditioner and buy a new bottle. Just trust me on this."

"Hey!" Hawkeye said. "No fair!"

In the morning, Kamala woke up feeling tired but happy. She had defeated the Inventor once again. And she felt more confident about her Super Hero life than she had in a long time. Talking to Thor had really helped.

But on her way to school, Kamala started to get worried. She'd still failed that Biology test, and that was still a big deal. Her parents were going to be so disappointed in her! Kamala had forgiven herself for screwing up the test, but she still hated having a bad grade on her record. She took pride in her schoolwork.

Plus, Nakia was probably still furious with her.

At lunch, Kamala sat by herself and pushed her french fries around on her plate gloomily.

"If you aren't going to eat those, give them to me," someone said. Kamala looked up and was surprised to see Nakia. She sat down and reached over delicately to snag one of Kamala's fries. Bruno plopped down next to her.

"Okay," Nakia said, biting into the fry, "you're officially forgiven, Kamala. I can't stand seeing you moping around like a big, sad puppy."

"Me neither," said Bruno, "which is why we talked to Mr. Lukoff on your behalf. And he's going to let you retake the test."

"Really?" Kamala said, astonished. "What did you tell him?"

"Bruno told him you spent the last week looking for someone's escaped pet bird," Nakia said.

"He was very impressed with your civic-mindedness," Bruno added.

Kamala was shocked. "But that's not true!" she said. "You can't just lie to a teacher like that!"

"Well," Bruno said thoughtfully, "you *were* being civic-minded."

"Huh," Kamala said. "I guess that's true." Then she and Bruno both froze and looked guiltily at Nakia. Nakia still didn't know about Ms. Marvel, and Kamala couldn't believe they'd come so close to letting something slip just then!

Nakia shrugged. "I'm sure you were," she said. "Just because I don't know what's going on with you doesn't mean I don't know there's *something* going on with you. I figure you'll tell me about it when you're ready. And in the meantime, you can retake that test and quit acting so sad."

"You really didn't have to—" Kamala started to say, but then she remembered what Thor had told her.

There's great honor in accepting help.

"Thank you," she told her friends. "This means a lot to me."

One week later, Kamala sat down to take a makeup exam in the Biology classroom. She had spent the entire week studying at Nakia's house, and she'd never felt better prepared for a test in her life. Her pencil flew across the page as she answered each question in turn with perfect confidence.

Finally, Kamala got to the extra-credit question at the bottom of the page. Kamala squinted. Something about this question was familiar. **Then she remembered!**

Extra Credit:
What is the term for an enzyme that divides nucleotides
—for example, in gene-splicing? + 3pts
NUCLEASE